Shiver Me Letters

A Pirate

A B C

Shiver Me Letters

A Pirate
A B C

SHIVER ME LETTERS
A PIRATE ABC

June Sobel   Illustrated by **Henry Cole**

SCHOLASTIC INC.
New York Toronto London Auckland Sydney
Mexico City New Delhi Hong Kong Buenos Aires

ISBN-13: 978-0-545-03776-1
ISBN-10: 0-545-03776-X

Text copyright © 2006 by June Sobel.
Illustrations copyright © 2006 by Henry Cole.
All rights reserved. Published by Scholastic Inc.,
557 Broadway, New York, NY 10012, by arrangement with Harcourt, Inc.
SCHOLASTIC and associated logos are trademarks and/or registered trademarks of Scholastic Inc.

12 11 10 9 8 7 6 5 4 3 2 1   7 8 9 10 11/0

Printed in the U.S.A.   40
This edition first printing, September 2007

The illustrations in this book were done in watercolor and ink on Arches hot press watercolor paper.
The display type was set in Belwe.
The text type was set in P22 1722.
Designed by April Ward

To my own pirates,
Mark and Adam **R.**
— **J. S.**

With love to Penoir
and Nancoir, my own
little Aruban pirate crew
—**H. C.**

They set up their sails
and followed the wind.
Spying an island,
they toothlessly
grinned.

"Land ho!"
yelled the pirates
as they rowed to the west.
"Capture those letters.
Let's make it our quest!"

Splash!

The anchor went into an **A**!

A B floated by on
the crystal clear bay.

In the sand sat a cannonball carved with a **C**!

They dug for doubloons and scooped up a **D**.

E escaped down from one pirate's pierced ear.

His mate raised a flag and found **F** —give a cheer!

In a chest glistened **G**,
all shiny and gold.

H hung from the hook
on a pirate of old.

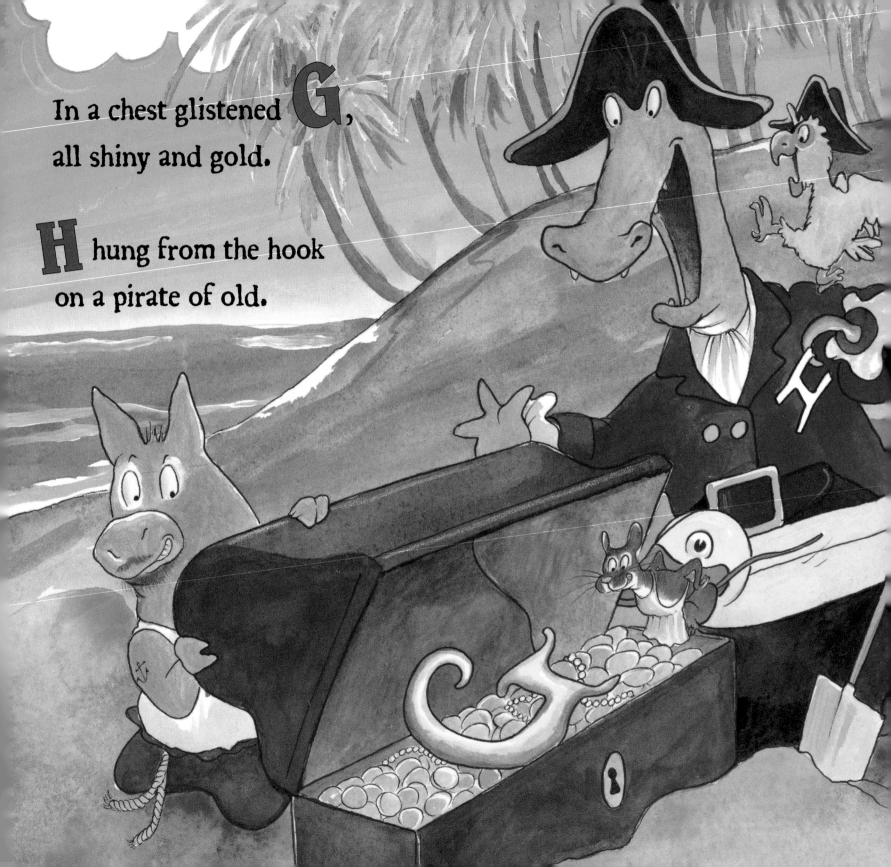

Ten paces north
stood a huge ivory I.

From out of the jungle, J jumped sky-high.

A **K** on a key slid under a shell.

Far from the water hid landlubber **L**.

A mysterious map with an **M** soon appeared,

while one nimble **N** popped right out of a beard!

They soon spotted  rolling into the ocean.

A parrot squawked, "P!"
What a commotion!

The gang questioned **Q** as it quacked in its nest.

"**R**," cried the crew.
"When do we rest?"

They saw **S** in the shape
of a swashbuckling sword,

then found **T** on a turtle as they hauled him aboard.

The crew dove underwater, caught **U** in a net.

They viewed **V** veiled in velvet, all soaking wet.

A wave washed up , sunburned and hot.

Pirates explored to find marked the spot!

They went to the captain
expecting a thanks.
They showed him the letters.
He showed them the planks.

"**R**," cried the crew. "Our work is not done.

We'll search and we'll plunder
to find the last one!"

And that very night
as they snored in their beds,
zillions of **Z**'s zoomed all over their heads.

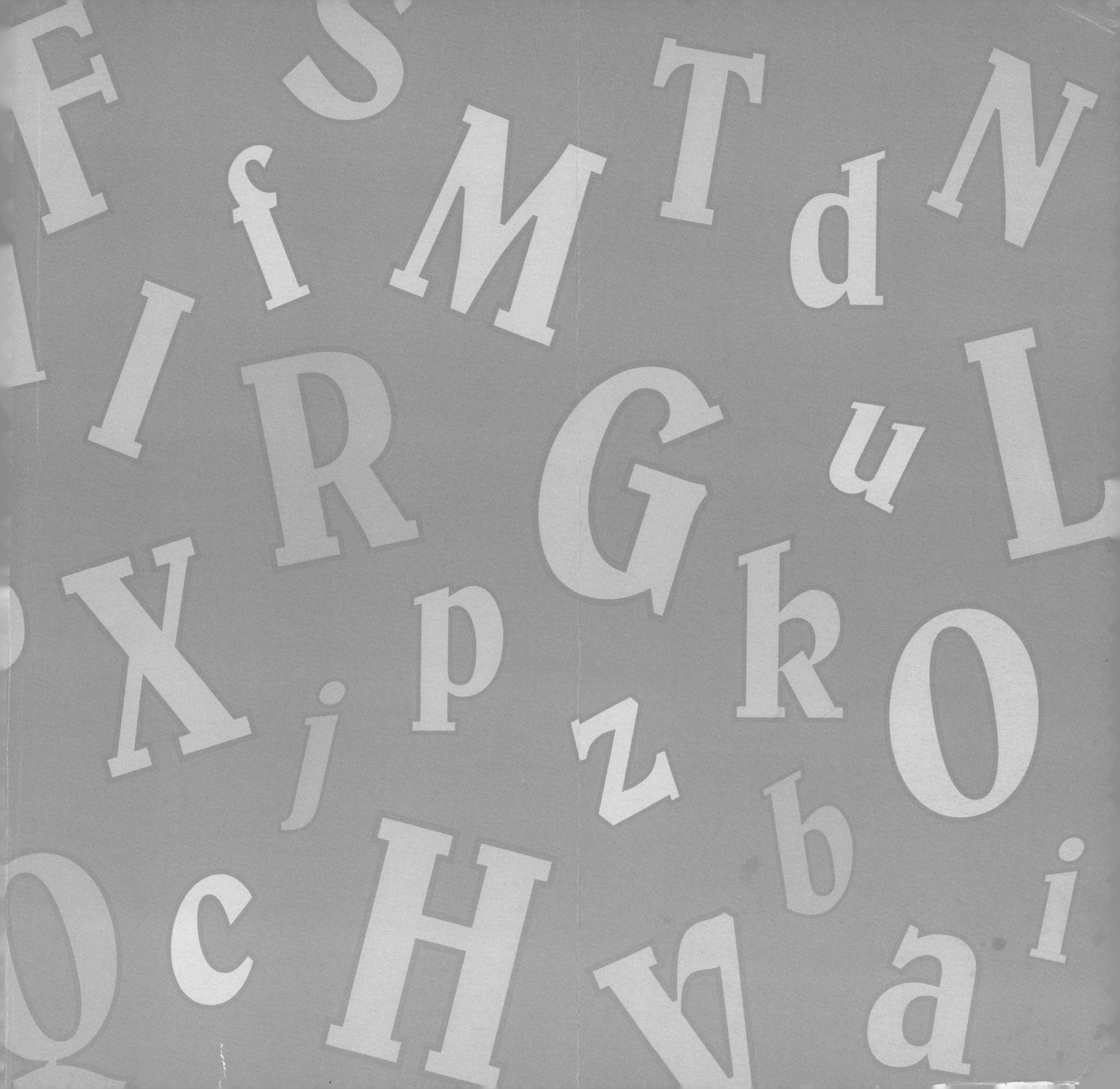